Is the Haunted House really haunted?

Plastic skeletons that shone in the dark were hanging from the ceiling. A tape of scary sounds was playing.

Eric whispered to Cam, "This is not very scary."

A door creaked open and they heard someone scream, "Oh! Help!"

"There is something scary ahead," Cam whispered.

Eric moved closer to Cam and Uncle George.

A toy black cat that almost looked real jumped off a bookcase shelf. It fell close to Cam and Eric. Then it stopped. It was held by a string.

"Oh, my!" Aunt Katie said.

Eric grabbed her hand, "I'm not scared," he said.

Then something dressed in black jumped at Aunt Katie.

"Oh! Help!" she screamed. "Let go of me!"

THE CAM JANSEN ADVENTURE SERIES
David A. Adler/Susanna Natti

Cam Jansen and the Mystery of the Stolen Diamonds

Cam Jansen and the Mystery of the U.F.O.

Cam Jansen and the Mystery of the Dinosaur Bones

Cam Jansen and the Mystery of the Television Dog

Cam Jansen and the Mystery of the Gold Coins

Cam Jansen and the Mystery of the Babe Ruth Baseball

Cam Jansen and the Mystery of the Circus Clown

Cam Jansen and the Mystery of the Monster Movie

Cam Jansen and the Mystery of the Carnival Prize

Cam Jansen and the Mystery of the Monkey House

Cam Jansen and the Mystery of the Stolen Corn Popper

Cam Jansen and the Mystery of Flight 54

Cam Jansen and the Mystery at the Haunted House

Cam Jansen and the Chocolate Fudge Mystery

Cam Jansen and the Triceratops Pops Mystery

Cam Jansen and the Ghostly Mystery

Cam Jansen and the Scary Snake Mystery

Cam Jansen and the Catnapping Mystery

Cam Jansen and the Barking Treasure Mystery

CAM JANSEN
and the Mystery at the Haunted House

★ ★

DAVID A. ADLER
Illustrated by Susanna Natti

★ ★

PUFFIN BOOKS

To Eitan.
With love
to a good boy
with a great smile

PUFFIN BOOKS
Published by the Penguin Group
Penguin Putnam Books for Young Readers,
345 Hudson Street, New York, New York 10014, U.S.A.
Penguin Books Ltd, 27 Wrights Lane, London W8 5TZ, England
Penguin Books Australia Ltd, Ringwood, Victoria, Australia
Penguin Books Canada Ltd, 10 Alcorn Avenue, Toronto, Ontario, Canada M4V 3B2
Penguin Books (N.Z.) Ltd, 182-190 Wairau Road, Auckland 10, New Zealand

Penguin Books Ltd, Registered Offices: Harmondsworth, Middlesex, England

First published by Viking Penguin,
a division of Penguin Books USA Inc., 1992
Published by Puffin Books, a division of Penguin Books USA Inc., 1994
Reissued 1999

1 3 5 7 9 10 8 6 4 2

THE LIBRARY OF CONGRESS HAS CATALOGED THE VIKING EDITION AS FOLLOWS:
Adler, David A.
Cam Jansen and the mystery of the haunted house / by David Adler;
illustrated by Susanna Natti p. cm.—(Cam Jansen adventure; 13)
Summary: Cam and her friend Eric chase the thief of Aunt Katie's wallet
through an amusement park and find themselves involved in another
case requiring their special detective skills.
ISBN 0-670-83419-X (hc.)
[1. Mystery and detective stories.] I. Natti, Susanna, ill.
II. Title. III. Series.
PZ7.A2615Cah 1992 [Fic]—dc20 91-28863 CIP AC

This edition ISBN 0-14-130649-1

Printed in the United States of America

RL: 2.1

Chapter One

Crash!

Eric Shelton was driving a small racing car in an amusement park. He turned and shouted to Cam Jansen, "Stop it! Stop crashing into me."

Eric held on to the steering wheel with both hands and gently pressed the pedal with his foot. The car moved slowly forward until it was close to the one ahead. Eric stepped lightly on the brake pedal. His car stopped.

Eric closed his eyes and clenched his teeth.

He knew Cam would move her car forward, too. He was sure she would crash into him.

Eric waited. Then he felt Cam's car softly touch his.

Eric turned and said, "That's better."

Eric moved his car up again and stopped. He unhooked the safety belt and stepped out onto the platform beside the racetrack.

Crash!

Cam had driven right into the back of Eric's car. She stepped out and met Eric at the exit.

"That was a great ride," Cam said.

Eric said, "It was fun until the end. Why did you keep bumping into me?"

"My pedal was loose. Anyway, the cars have those big bumpers because they expect us to crash."

It was a warm spring Sunday afternoon. Cam and Eric were in the park with Cam's Aunt Katie and Uncle George.

"There they are," Cam said. She pointed

to two old people sitting on a bench. Aunt Katie was talking to a woman pushing a baby carriage. Uncle George was holding a cane and resting. His eyes were closed and his legs were stretched out in front of him.

"Isn't she just the cutest baby?" Aunt Katie said to Cam.

"Yes, she's very cute." Cam looked around and asked, "What ride are we going on next?"

"Look at her hair. Look at those tiny curls."

"I see her hair, Aunt Katie. It's very nice," Cam said. Then she whispered, "Eric has a baby brother named Howie. I can see him any time I want, but this is the only chance I'll have to take these rides."

Aunt Katie stood and said, "You're right. I told you we would go on every ride we can, and we will. Where should we go next?"

Cam closed her eyes and said, "*Click.*"

"What is she doing?" the woman with the baby carriage asked.

Eric explained, "Cam has a photographic memory. She can take one look at something and remember it perfectly. It's as if she has a mental camera, and photographs stored in her head. Whenever she wants to remember something, she says, '*Click*.' That's the sound her mental camera makes."

Aunt Katie told the woman, "When Cam was a baby, we called her Jennifer. That's her real name. But as soon as we found out about her amazing memory, we began calling her 'The Camera.' Soon, 'The Camera' was shortened to 'Cam.' "

"I'm looking at a picture of the map we saw when we came into the park," Cam said. Her eyes were still closed. "If we go up the road to the left, we'll pass the parachute and train rides, and the Haunted House. To the right are the merry-go-round, pony rides, and the gift shop."

"Amazing," the woman with the baby carriage said.

"Watch out!" Eric called.

Cam opened her eyes.

Two teenage boys on roller skates were

coming toward Cam, Eric, Aunt Katie, and the woman with the baby.

Cam moved to the left. Eric and the woman moved to the right. Aunt Katie didn't know which way to go. First she moved to the right. Then she moved to the left.

Crash!

One of the boys couldn't stop. He went right into Aunt Katie.

"Oh, my!" she said as she fell to the ground.

The boys tried to help her, but they couldn't. Each time they started to pull her up, they rolled on their skates and fell again. Finally Cam, Eric, and Uncle George helped her to the bench.

"Oh, my," Aunt Katie said as she sat down.

"We're very sorry," the boys said. Then they rolled down the road toward the parachute ride.

Aunt Katie brushed off her clothes. Uncle George helped her.

"Are you hurt?" Eric asked.

Aunt Katie smiled and said, "No, I'm fine. Let's go to the next ride. Let's go to the Haunted House."

"Oh, yes," Eric said. "I like to be scared."

Cam puffed out her cheeks. She held her hands over her head, waved them, and yelled, "Boo!"

Uncle George held his hands to his heart.

Aunt Katie said, "Oh, my!"

Eric said, "They're just being nice. You're not scary at all."

"Well, then, let's go to the Haunted House," Aunt Katie said. "I'm sure it will be *very* scary."

Chapter Two

Cam, Eric, Aunt Katie, and Uncle George walked up the road to the left.

"Wa! Wa!"

"Oh, look, there's a baby crying," Cam said. She and Eric walked quickly ahead.

"Why are you crying?" Cam asked the little girl.

"Wa! Wa!"

"She lost her balloon," the child's mother said. "It's caught in the tree. I tied it to her stroller. Somehow it came off."

Cam said, "If I stand on the bench, maybe I can reach it."

"You might fall," Aunt Katie said. "I think you should call one of the guards."

"We could get a ladder," Eric said.

Uncle George turned his cane around. With the curved end he caught the loop on the string and pulled the balloon down. He gave it to the child.

"Oh, thank you," the child's mother said.

Uncle George touched his cap, smiled, and walked ahead.

"He doesn't talk much, does he," Eric whispered to Cam.

"Uncle George says it's a noisy world. He says most people talk too much and too loud."

"Oh, my," Aunt Katie said. The teenage boys were skating toward them. Aunt Katie and Uncle George went quickly to the side of the road and let them skate past.

"They shouldn't be allowed to race around here like that," Aunt Katie said.

Cam, Eric, Aunt Katie, and Uncle George walked to the Haunted House. They waited at the end of a long line outside the entrance.

A group was let into the house. Cam, Eric, and the others moved forward until they were near a large sign. Cam read it aloud.

WARNING.

SMALL CHILDREN AND

NERVOUS ADULTS KEEP OUT!

INSIDE ARE SUDDEN

NOISES AND SCARY EFFECTS.

ENTER AT YOUR OWN RISK.

"Maybe we should try the merry-go-round instead," Aunt Katie said.

"We're not small children," Eric told her. "We're ten years old."

"I want to go in," Cam said as she ran her fingers through her hair. She has what people call bright red hair, even though it is more orange than red. Eric's hair is dark brown.

The exit door opened. A girl holding her mother's hand came out smiling. "That was great," she said.

A few more people came out. They were smiling, talking, and laughing. Then a woman in a blue dress came out holding her hand to her chest. "That was scary," she said. "I was never so scared in all my life."

Cam, Eric, and the others watched her walk to a bench and sit down.

"She looks terrible," Aunt Katie said. "Maybe we shouldn't go in."

HAUNT
EXIT

The entrance door opened. The guard standing there said, “Let’s go. Move ahead. We have room inside for a few more people.”

Cam, Eric, and the others moved closer to the entrance.

“Are you together?” the guard asked.

“Yes,” Cam said.

“OK. All four of you can go in. The rest of you will have to wait.”

The door closed behind Cam, Eric, Aunt Katie, and Uncle George. It was dark inside the house. They followed dim purple lights past a painting with moving eyes.

A low, deep voice said, “Welcome to my home.”

“Oh, my,” Aunt Katie said.

Plastic skeletons that shone in the dark were hanging from the ceiling. A tape of scary sounds was playing.

Eric whispered to Cam, “This is not very scary.”

A door creaked open and they heard someone scream, “Oh! Help!”

“There is something scary ahead,” Cam whispered.

Eric moved closer to Cam and Uncle George.

A toy black cat that almost looked real jumped off a bookcase shelf. It fell close to Cam and Eric. Then it stopped. It was held by a string.

“Oh, my!” Aunt Katie said.

Eric grabbed her hand. “I’m not scared,” he said.

Then something dressed in black jumped at Aunt Katie.

“Oh! Help!” she screamed. “Let go of me!”

Chapter Three

Aunt Katie reached for Uncle George and held onto his hand. They followed the small purple lights past spiderwebs and creaking furniture. A chair walked past them. The walls seemed to be falling in.

Cam, Eric, Aunt Katie, and Uncle George walked faster. A door opened. They were outside the Haunted House.

"Oh, my," Aunt Katie said. "That was scary, but I liked it."

"That wasn't so scary," Eric said, "but I liked it, too."

"Did you see that?" a woman behind them asked. "Something jumped right out at me." She opened her handbag and took out a candy. "Would you like one?"

"No, thank you," Cam said.

"I need something, but not candy," Aunt Katie said. "I need a cup of hot tea."

Cam closed her eyes and said, "*Click.*"

"There's a refreshment stand just past the log ride," Cam said. She opened her eyes. "Follow me."

"Will you look at that!" Aunt Katie said when they reached the refreshment stand. "We even have to wait in line to buy a drink."

Aunt Katie and Uncle George stood at the end of the line. Cam and Eric went to the log ride. They watched people sitting in cut-out logs slide into a large pool of water.

"That looks like fun," Eric said. "Maybe we can do that next."

Cam and Eric walked back to the refreshment stand. Aunt Katie and Uncle George were still near the end of the line.

"Tell me what you want to eat," Aunt Katie said. "This is the only chance we'll have for refreshments. I won't wait in this line again."

Cam and Eric looked at the list of items being sold. "I'd like to have some orange juice and pretzels," Cam said.

"Please, could I have a vanilla ice cream pop?" Eric asked.

"Hmm," Aunt Katie said. "Vanilla tea for

me, an orange pop for George, coffee and pretzels for Cam. And what did you want, Eric?"

"I want a vanilla pop."

"I'm all mixed up," Aunt Katie said. "Why don't you wait until it's our turn. Then you can all tell me what you want."

The line moved slowly. When they reached the counter, the man there asked, "What would you like?"

"I want tea with lemon. I know that," Aunt Katie said. "And George wants a regular coffee."

Cam and Eric told the man what they wanted. He put it all on a cardboard tray and brought it to the counter. He told Aunt Katie what everything cost.

Aunt Katie opened her handbag and reached in. Then she looked inside her handbag. She took out something wrapped in aluminum foil, a small note pad, and some pencils and gave them to Cam to hold.

"Please," the man behind the counter said. "There are other people waiting."

"I can't find my wallet," Aunt Katie told him.

Uncle George paid for the refreshments. He carried them from the counter to a table. Cam, Eric, and Aunt Katie followed him. As Aunt Katie walked to the table, she was still looking in her handbag.

Aunt Katie took the pencils, note pad, and the small package wrapped in foil back from Cam. She put the pencils and note pad in her handbag.

"Maybe my wallet is in here," she said. She unwrapped the foil. Inside was a jelly sandwich.

"Oh, my," Aunt Katie said. "My wallet *is* gone. I know I had it when we came into the park. I paid for the entrance tickets."

Aunt Katie took a bite of the jelly sandwich and then wrapped it in the foil again. "Or did you pay for the tickets?" she asked Uncle George. "Maybe I left my wallet at home."

"No," Uncle George said. "You paid for the tickets." He took Aunt Katie's hand and said, "Let's go. We have to find that wallet."

Chapter Four

"He spoke!" Eric whispered.

Aunt Katie quickly drank her tea and went with Uncle George. Cam and Eric ran to catch up with them.

"Where are you going?" Cam asked.

"We're looking for one of the park policemen," Aunt Katie said. "I saw one here before. He wore a nice blue uniform, had a badge on, and carried a walkie-talkie."

"I think you should go to the park entrance," Eric said. "That's the last place you remember having your wallet. My father

once left his wallet at the ticket booth of a movie theater."

"Look," Cam said, "there's a police officer."

Cam ran to the officer. She came back a few minutes later and told Aunt Katie, "She says we should go to the security office. She told me where it is. Follow me."

The security office was in a small building near the merry-go-round. Cam, Eric, Aunt Katie, and Uncle George went inside.

"Oh, my," Aunt Katie said. "There's a line here, too." Aunt Katie and Uncle George got in line, right behind a woman in a blue dress.

Cam and Eric went to the park entrance. Many people were coming into the park. Cam tried to push one of the turnstiles to go out. A man on the other side was pushing it in.

"It doesn't go that way," the man said.

"Come on," Eric said. "We have to go through the gate over there. But first we have to get our hands stamped, so we can come back in."

At the gate, a woman pressed a rubber stamp onto an ink pad and then onto the backs of Cam's and Eric's hands.

"There's nothing on my hand," Cam said.

The woman said, "Yes, there is. When

you're ready to come back into the park, I'll pass your hands under a special light. Then you'll see what I stamped. You'll be surprised."

Cam and Eric walked through the gate. Cam was still looking at her hand.

There were several ticket booths. Eric pointed to one and said, "This is it. This is where Aunt Katie bought the tickets. It had the shortest line."

Cam and Eric walked to the front of the line. A man surrounded with children was next.

"We don't want to buy tickets," Eric told the man.

"I don't want to buy tickets, either. But it's the only way to get into the park."

"We were already in the park," Eric said. "Look at my hand. It's stamped."

The man looked at Eric's hand and smiled. "There's nothing on your hand, but you can go ahead of me."

TICKETS
TICKET

Cam closed her eyes and said, "*Click.*"

Eric said to the ticket seller, "My friend's aunt was here about two hours ago. We think she may have left her wallet."

"*Click.*"

"I have a credit card that someone forgot, and two pens, a newspaper, and a magazine, but no wallet."

"Eric," Cam said, "Eric, I know where Aunt Katie's wallet is. She didn't leave it somewhere. It was stolen and I know who took it."

Chapter Five

"Who was it? Who stole her wallet?" Eric asked.

"Those roller-skating boys, the ones who knocked Aunt Katie down. They took it. Pickpockets work like that, in teams. They bump into people and reach into their pockets or handbags. Come on. We have to find them."

Cam walked to the turnstiles.

"May I have your ticket, please?" the guard standing there said.

"We were in already. Our hands were stamped."

The guard pointed to the left and said, "You have to go to the re-entry gate."

Cam and Eric ran to the gate.

"You're back here so soon," the woman there said. "Now you'll see what I stamped on your hand. Every day I use a different stamp."

She held Cam's hand under a small lamp.

"It's a frog sitting on a lily pad," Cam said.

"Yesterday I used my stamp of a rabbit eating a carrot."

Eric passed his hand under the lamp. Then he asked Cam, "Where do we look for them?"

"They were skating along this path. They probably still are."

Cam and Eric walked past a popcorn wagon, a shop selling posters and post-cards, and the racing car ride. Cam was walking quickly. Eric had to hurry to keep up with her.

"Why are we looking for them?" Eric asked. "Why don't we just tell one of the guards? They have walkie-talkies. They could find the boys real fast."

Cam turned while she was walking and told Eric, "Because I don't know for sure that they stole the wallet. I *clicked*, but I don't have a picture of them taking it."

"Watch it! Watch where you're going," a man said. Cam had bumped into him.

"I'm sorry," Cam said. She walked more slowly now, and looked ahead as she spoke to Eric.

"We'll follow them. As soon as they knock into someone, we'll check if his wallet is missing. If it is, we'll know those boys are the thieves. Then we'll tell the guards."

Eric smiled. "Did *you* take his wallet?"

"Whose?"

"That man you bumped into. We're a team. We're walking together and you bumped into that man. Did you take his wallet?"

"Of course not! But that's why we have to see what happens when those skaters bump into someone else. Maybe I'm wrong."

Cam and Eric walked past small shops selling magic tricks, stuffed animals, and children's books. They walked past the Spinning Hat ride and a very long line of people waiting to ride the roller coaster.

Suddenly Cam ran ahead, pointing and shouting. "Look! Look! There they are!"

The two boys were skating on a path around a small pond. There were ducks, geese, and a few swans in the pond. Cam ran after the boys. Eric followed her.

The boys skated past a woman and her two children. They skated between a man and his son.

Cam almost bumped into the man. "Excuse me," she said.

"Excuse me, too," Eric said.

The boys skated past a man who was throwing bread crumbs to the ducks, geese, and swans. The noise of the skates scared them and a few of the ducks flew off.

Eric stopped running. He sat on a bench and stretched out his legs. When Cam saw him there, she stopped, too.

"I can't keep up with them," Eric said to Cam.

"Neither can I."

They sat on the bench and watched the boys skate around the pond. A few people had to move quickly to get out of their way. One woman yelled at the boys, but they didn't stop. They skated faster and faster until they knocked into a man selling balloons. When he fell to the ground, one of his balloons flew off.

Cam jumped up from the bench. "You help the man," she told Eric. "Then check if his wallet has been stolen. I'll get someone from security."

One of the boys reached out his hand and said to the man, "Let me help you up."

SPINNING HAT

The man pushed his hand away and said, "Don't help me. Just take off those skates. You boys are a danger."

"I'll help you," Eric said.

The man reached out and held onto Eric's hand and pulled himself up.

"We're sorry," one of the boys said. Then both boys skated off.

Cam ran past the shops. Then, near the Spinning Hat ride, she saw a security guard. Just as Cam reached the guard, the boys skated past.

Trill. Trill.

The guard blew his whistle. He ran after the boys. Cam followed him.

"Stop that! Stop skating."

The guard couldn't keep up with the boys. He waved his arms at them, but they didn't seem to notice. The guard stopped running. He took the walkie-talkie off his belt, and spoke into it.

"This is Frankie in Section Four. Two

teenage boys just skated past me toward the roller coaster. Maybe you can stop them. I couldn't."

"They bumped into my aunt," Cam told the guard. "They knocked her down and . . ."

"Wait! Wait!"

Cam turned. Eric was running toward her.

"Don't tell him!" he called out. "Don't tell him!"

Chapter Six

When Eric reached Cam, he took a deep breath and said, "They didn't take his wallet. The man still has it."

The guard was a tall, thin man. He looked down at Cam and asked, "Do you have something else to tell me?"

"No."

The guard spoke into his walkie-talkie again. "This is Frankie in Section Four. I'm going back to my post," he said. Then he walked back to the Spinning Hat ride.

"What do we do now?" Eric asked.

“Let’s go back to the security office. Aunt Katie and Uncle George may be worried about us.”

They walked past the Spinning Hat ride. Children sitting in the hats were laughing and shouting as they spun around. People on the log ride and on the merry-go-round seemed to be having a good time, too.

“You know,” Eric said, “every time I go someplace with you, something seems to happen. I’d rather spin around in a hat, or sit in a log floating in water than chase two boys on roller skates.”

Aunt Katie and Uncle George had answered some questions and signed some papers, but they hadn't found the wallet. They were outside the security office waiting for Cam and Eric.

"We won't let this ruin our day," Aunt Katie said. "Let's go on some more rides. When we're ready to leave the park, we'll stop at the Lost and Found department. I'm sure my wallet will turn up."

Eric said, "I'd like to go on the Spinning Hat ride. It looks like lots of fun and I know just where it is."

As they followed him to the ride, Aunt Katie said, "I wasn't the only one who lost a wallet today. The woman just ahead of me in line lost her wallet, too."

Cam stopped walking. She closed her eyes and said, "*Click.*"

Eric, Aunt Katie, and Uncle George stopped and watched Cam.

"*Click.*"

"*Click.*"

Cam opened her eyes. She smiled and walked ahead.

Cam stopped when they came to the Haunted House. "Let's go through here again," she said. "It was fun before and the line is short now."

Eric did not want to go through the house again, but Cam insisted. After a few minutes, the doors opened and they went inside.

Eric smiled at the painting with the moving eyes. When the low, deep voice said, "Welcome to my home," Eric said, "Thank you."

A door creaked open. Someone screamed, "Help! Help!" Then a toy black cat jumped off the shelf at them. Eric waved his arms at the cat and yelled, "Boo!"

"Oh, my," Aunt Katie said. "You didn't scare the cat, but you did scare me."

They followed the small purple lights past spiderwebs and creaking furniture. The

chair walked past them again and the walls seemed to be falling down. Then a door opened and they were outside.

"That wasn't as scary the second time," Aunt Katie said.

"It wasn't scary at all," Eric said. "Now let's go to the spinning hats. That will be fun."

Eric started to walk ahead.

"Stop!" Uncle George called. "Where's Cam?"

Aunt Katie and Eric looked around.

"Oh, my," Aunt Katie said. "She never came out of that house."

Chapter Seven

Aunt Katie went to the guard standing by the exit and said, "My niece went through with us and she's still in there. She may be lost, or hurt."

"How old is she?"

"Ten."

"She's old enough to follow the lights. Don't worry. No one gets lost in the house. Some people just take longer than others to go through it."

Eric, Aunt Katie, and Uncle George waited outside the exit door. Some of the people coming out of the Haunted House looked scared. Others came out smiling and laughing.

Aunt Katie looked at her watch.

The door opened. More people came out, but Cam wasn't with them.

Aunt Katie looked at her watch again. Uncle George patted her hand and said, "Don't worry."

Aunt Katie took a few steps to the left. She turned and took a few steps to the right. As she walked, she talked. "Maybe she fell. Maybe the black cat scared her, or the moving eyes, and she fainted. I'm going back in there. I'm getting in line and going back in."

Just then the door opened. A woman, two children, a young man, and Cam came out of the house.

Aunt Katie ran to her. "Oh, I was so worried," she told Cam.

"Shh!"

"I thought you were hurt, or maybe lost."

"Shh!" Cam said again and pointed to the young man ahead.

He was wearing a black shirt, black pants, and black shoes. He was carrying a small shopping bag.

Cam followed him through the crowd. Eric, Aunt Katie, and Uncle George followed Cam. When they came to the main path, where there was more room to walk, Cam didn't follow the young man as closely.

"Get one of the security guards," Cam whispered to Eric. "He's the one who stole Aunt Katie's wallet. He stole lots of other people's wallets, too."

Eric and Aunt Katie went into the security office. Cam and Uncle George followed the man through the gate to the parking lot.

The young man went to a small green car. He opened the trunk and emptied the shopping bag into it. He looked around and then walked back toward Cam and Uncle George.

Uncle George didn't want the young man to know he was watching him. He quickly went to one of the public telephones. He picked up the receiver and talked into it. "Yes, Ruthie."

The man walked past Cam and Uncle George to the re-entry gate.

"Shouldn't we follow him?" Uncle George whispered.

"We don't have to. I know just where he's

ENTRANCE
TICKETS
TELEPHONES

going." Cam smiled. "You can finish your telephone call to Ruthie."

"What?" Uncle George looked at the telephone he was still holding. "Oh," he said, and hung up.

Cam waited a minute. Then she said, "We can go now."

At the re-entry gate, Cam passed her hand under the small lamp. The woman said to Uncle George, "You're lucky. I remember you so you can go in again, but you should have had your hand stamped. Take a look at the stamp I used today. It's cute."

Cam passed her hand under the small lamp again. Uncle George looked at it. "It's a frog sitting on a lily pad," Cam said.

Cam and Uncle George met Eric and Aunt Katie outside the security office. Two security guards were with them. One guard was short and had a long curly beard. The other guard was a woman with long blonde hair.

Cam said to them,"I'll bet a lot of people came to you today and told you their wallets had been stolen."

"Yes."

"Well, if you follow me, I'll take you to the thief. I know just where he's hiding."

Chapter Eight

They all followed Cam to the Haunted House. Cam walked quickly. She also talked quickly.

"Aunt Katie gave me the first clue. She said the woman ahead of her at the security office had lost her wallet, too. Well, I said, *Click*. I had seen that woman with the blue dress before. I had a picture of her stored in my head. She was the same scared woman we saw coming out of the Haunted House.

"I said *Click* again. I remembered that someone jumped out at Aunt Katie. He

must have jumped out at that woman, too. That's why she was so scared.

"People thought the man dressed in black was there to scare them. He wasn't. He hid in the dark and stole from them. I watched him do it."

They had reached the Haunted House. The guards walked to the front of the line with Cam. The short guard went to the exit door. The guard with the long blonde hair told the guard at the house not to let anyone in.

They waited for people to leave the Haunted House. Then the guard with the blonde hair said to Cam, "I'm Mary. Can you show me where the thief is hiding?"

Cam and Mary walked into the Haunted House. Mary turned on the lights.

"He's not in here," Cam said. "He's in the next room."

Cam followed Mary through the creaking door. Mary turned on the light.

"There he is," Cam said and pointed. "Behind that curtain."

The man dressed in black ran for the exit. Mary and Cam ran after him. The door opened. The man ran out, right into the arms of the short guard with the curly beard.

Cam told Mary and the other guard that she and Uncle George had followed him to the parking lot. "You'll probably find Aunt Katie's wallet and all the other missing wallets in the trunk of the green car."

The guards told Aunt Katie that as soon as they found her wallet, she would be called to the security office. “While you wait,” Mary said, “why don’t you go on one of the rides.”

The thief was locked in handcuffs and led away by the two guards. Cam, Eric, Aunt Katie, and Uncle George watched them walk off. Then they walked to the Spinning Hat ride.

"You know," Uncle George said as they walked, "Aunt Katie and I are very proud of you." Uncle George stopped walking for a moment. He patted Cam's hand, looked at her, smiled, and said, "That's all I'm going to say."

"Thank you," Cam said. "Many people talk too much, but you say just enough. I'm glad you're proud of me."

Cam and Eric went on the Spinning Hat ride. Aunt Katie and Uncle George stood on the side and watched.

Cam and Eric rode in an upside down purple derby. In the center of the derby was a large metal wheel. The more they turned the wheel, the faster the hat spun around. Cam kept turning the wheel. When Cam and Eric came off the ride, they were dizzy.

"Oh, my," Aunt Katie said. "You're walking funny."

"May I have your attention, please," someone announced over the park's loudspeaker.

"Would Stanley Johnson, Alyse Neumark, Gabriella Goldwyn, Pat Baker, and Jessica Jones please come to the security office. Thank you."

"Their wallets must have been found in that man's trunk," Cam said. "Let's start walking toward the office. I'm sure Aunt Katie's name will be announced soon."

As they walked through the park, they passed two teenage boys. Each boy was carrying a pair of roller skates.

"I guess someone finally stopped them from skating," Eric said.

"May I have your attention, please. Would Jane Taylor, Adina Zellner, Karen Kessler, and Katie Jansen please come to the security office. Thank you."

"That's me! That's me!" Aunt Katie said. "They found my wallet."

There was a crowd of people at the security office. The thief was there, too, along with several police officers. Aunt Katie's wallet was returned to her. Then Mary and a woman wearing a fancy flower-print dress came over to meet Cam.

"This is the girl I told you about," Mary said to the woman. "She found the thief."

The woman held out her hand to Cam and said, "I'm the owner of this park. My name is Dana Moore. I'm very grateful to you."

Dana Moore was holding an envelope. She gave it to Cam and said, "I'm sure that while you were chasing that thief, you missed some rides. I'm giving you four passes to come into the park as often as you want this month, for free."

Cam thanked Dana Moore.

"That's great," Eric said. "We can come here during spring vacation."

"Uncle George and I would be happy to take you," Aunt Katie said.

Eric said, "Maybe then we can spend the whole day going on rides. Maybe Cam won't

EXIT
AMUSE
PARK

find some mystery to solve or some thief to chase."

Cam looked at Aunt Katie and Uncle George and said, "Maybe." Then she turned to Eric, smiled, and said, "And maybe not."